To Mum & Dad — TA

OXFORD
UNIVERSITY PRESS

Great Clarendon Street, Oxford OX2 6DP
Oxford University Press is a department of the University of Oxford.
It furthers the University's objective of excellence in research, scholarship,
and education by publishing worldwide. Oxford is a registered trade mark
of Oxford University Press in the UK and in certain other countries

First published 2020

British Library Cataloguing in Publication Data

Data available

ISBN: 978-0-19-277515-3

1 3 5 7 9 10 8 6 4 2

Printed in India

Graph paper: Alfonso de Tomas/Shutterstock.com

Written by
TIM ALLMAN

Drawn by
NICK SHEPHERD

MAX
AGAINST
EXTINCTION

Changing the world one
placard at a time

OXFORD
UNIVERSITY PRESS

'I don't think I can just go back to

normal again,' I announced to my

friends in the playground.

'What do you mean?' laughed Nish.

'When have you ever been normal?'

'Maybe you haven't noticed, but I'm

pretty keen on trying to **save the planet!**' I said.

It's true, you don't talk about much else these days added Tessa.

I don't know about that!

Nish chimed in. 'The other day,

you tried to make us guess what

you'd had for dinner for ages. Then,

you talked for hours about the new Gerbil

Hero! film.'

'Pineapple double pizza

2

sandwich, remember? And yes, the film is awesome!' I agreed. 'But that doesn't matter right now. Ever since we did all that stuff for that green competition on TV, I've been trying to make a new **Plan for the Planet.'**

'We've done a lot already, Max,' said Tessa. 'We did loads to **green up** the school.'

'But we need more!' I said, walking round in circles and waving my arms for emphasis.

'I feel I've changed, and other things aren't changing fast enough!' I pulled out my phone to show my friends some pictures. 'Look at this!'

'Who are these kids?' asked Nish, eyes scanning the photos I'd posted.

Greta, duh!

'Everyone knows Greta!' said Tessa,
pointing at her picture. 'But I don't recognize
the others.'

'Yes, Greta from Sweden, of course; and
Aditya from India, and Nina from Ecuador,
and Mari from the USA ...' I pointed them
out. '... and loads of others. They're all kids
who have been in the news for **fighting**
for the planet.'

'You've been on TV already too, Max,' said
Nish.

'It's not about having your fifteen

minutes of fame!' I said. 'There are millions

of kids doing stuff around the world who

we never hear about. And we can be part

of it — I just can't work out what to do next.

With environmental stuff, there's so much to

worry about. I feel anxious if I'm not doing

something about it. When I am,

I feel great!'

'You can campaign to stop **my dad's

farts** if you like,' suggested Nish. 'They are

an environmental hazard!'

We all laughed, then Tessa spoke. 'You'll come up with a plan, Max. It's what you do best.'

'Well, I've got a whole day of school to come up with my next plan,' I agreed. 'As long as the teachers don't distract me by making me work, it will be fine.'

I tried talking to Tessa and Nish about my

new ideas on the way home, but Tessa was

 more interested in talking about **crisps**.

Apparently, she knew a shop which had a new

flavour she was keen to try, so we went off to

find that.

BRAND NEW!!

CR SPS

As we left the shop, munching crisps, I wasn't sure the detour had been worth it.

'I don't think much of this cabbage and mustard flavour,' Nish admitted.

'No. I'm sticking to salt and vinegar,' I agreed. 'Hey, let's go down Meadow Lane. That's a nice way back.'

I led the way into the road, but stopped in my tracks as we rounded the corner.

'What's up, Max?' asked Tessa. I stood and pointed.

'That fence, that's what's up! It wasn't there last week. Something's going on.'

There was a new wire-mesh fence all along the other side of the road, separating the pavement from the land beyond it. I quickly crossed the road to read the signs which had been fixed to the fence. As I did so, my heart sank.

SCOLEX DEVELOPMENT CORPORATION, COMING SOON-'MEADOW GREEN', PRESTIGE OFFICE SPACES, PLANNING PERMISSION PENDING

'I don't believe it!' I exclaimed, shaking

my head in horror. Tessa and Nish walked

over to join me. 'These **whiffheads**

want to build an office block here, on this

beautiful place!' I continued, shaking my

head furiously. 'As if there aren't enough

offices in the world already.'

'I'm not sure it's beautiful exactly, Max,'

said Tessa. 'I mean, you're totally right about

there being enough offices,' she added quickly. 'My dad's always moaning about people in the office, saying they need to get out into the real world.'

'This IS the real world, Tessa!' I said.

'Remember coming here before, Nish?'

'Yes! My trainers got soaked, and I got **thorns in my bum!'** Nish frowned.

'Nature can be harsh sometimes,'

I said. We all stood in silence, staring

through the mesh of the fence at

the land beyond. We saw a mass of

brambles and scrubby trees, with gaps

revealing a tussocky wet field. The

edge nearest us was littered with old

cans, and torn plastic bags fluttered

limply from tree branches.

I could see why it might not look beautiful to Tessa, but I knew it was important. We called it 'the Bramble Field', but there was much more to it. About a year ago, I'd explored it with Nish, weaving through the scrub to find the meadow behind. Nish hadn't liked it, and had moaned because he got wet feet, but I thought it was great. There were lots of flowers I didn't know the names of, and frogs and newts in the ponds, and more insects buzzing around than I'd seen anywhere else in

our town.

'It might not look much, but it's

like a little nature reserve!'

I proclaimed. 'Wild places

are really important,

especially in towns. These offices must not be

built!'

Tessa nodded sadly. 'It's a shame, but it's

too late.'

'Sorry, but I don't think you can win this

one, Max,' Nish agreed.

'_No way!_' I exclaimed, turning away from the fence. My mind was racing as I paced up and down the pavement. 'Remember all the photos of the kids I showed you, all fighting for the planet? What would they do now? They wouldn't just give up!'

I'd been trying to think of a new **Plan for the Planet,** and this was going to be it. We were going to save the Bramble Field!

I rushed the rest of the way home, mind filling up with plans. The first stage in any campaign is to SPREAD THE WORD. So, after tea that evening, I decided to make some signs and placards.

There were some old cardboard boxes under

18

the stairs, and it didn't take long to empty

the stuff out of them and cut them up. Next,

I borrowed some of my little sister Lily's

brushes and paints, went up to my room, and

started thinking about what to write.

I needed some good slogans that got the message across. I decided that a biscuit or two (or maybe three . . .) might help me concentrate, so I went down to the kitchen.

Mum was in there, reading a glossy brochure. Ah, Max! We've been talking about summer plans she said. 'We haven't

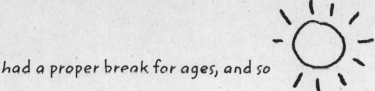

had a proper break for ages, and so

we're going abroad on holiday this year.

Somewhere sunny!'

'I can't think about holidays right now,

Mum,' I replied. 'I'm planning a NEW

CAMPAIGN. They want to build offices on

the Bramble Field, and we have to stop them!'

Mum wrinkled her nose like she'd smelt

something weird, but didn't know what it

was. 'Are you sure, Max? Your big ideas

usually end up with trouble. I don't think the

21

headteacher has forgiven you for getting

everyone to run out of school last term.'

'We didn't run, we walked!' I objected. 'It

was a climate strike! We should do that again

one day . . . anyway, this time it's nothing to

do with the school, so we won't get in trouble.'

Mum looked dubious. 'Hmmm. You'd

better not! Anyway, look at these!'

She pushed the pile of holiday brochures

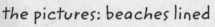

towards me. I flicked through

the pictures: beaches lined

with palm trees, sparkling swimming pools,

people lying on sun-loungers, and a grinning

man holding a lobster, for some reason.

'It looks OK, but I think I'd just get bored.

And I'm not getting involved with lobsters,' I

said firmly.

'Lobsters are optional!' Mum grinned.

'Come on, you wouldn't get bored. The hotel runs a kids' club. That's the best bit — you and Lily can do your own thing in the kids' club all day, while your dad and I just . . . RELAX. We need a proper rest! We haven't been away for years, and there's a deal on cheap flights right now . . .'

Mum went on for ages about her holiday plans. It distracted me, and I didn't manage to get any more placard-making done that evening.

I'd been looking forward to the end of term because the summer holidays are always better than being in school, and I'd wanted to have some time to make more plans for the planet – but, as I got ready for bed, the idea of an actual holiday ran round my mind. I'd had a busy time, after all, with all my campaigning at school over the last few months.

I went to sleep quite quickly, and was

Z Z Z z

soon dreaming. This often happens when I've

got a lot going on in my head, and it's not

always nice. This was a good dream, though.

It started in school, but instead of sitting on

a chair I was on a big pink flamingo-shaped

lilo. No one else noticed, even when I flew out

of the classroom window on the flamingo,

and then shifted to floating around a big

swimming pool—but filled with lemonade

instead of water. I was lounging on the lilo in

shades, getting a suntan, eating 20 flavours

The next morning, I was still daydreaming

about sun, sea and ice cream but I needed to

stop thinking about the holiday (even though

it was going to be fantastic!)

Hissssssss

and concentrate on our

goal. If we managed

of ice cream (out of a bike helmet for some

reason, but never mind). Super-cool! This

is the life, I thought—perhaps I did need a

holiday . . .

to save the Bramble Field, I'd have earned

a holiday for sure! I hadn't got very far

with my placard-making, so I decided to

do it in school instead, where I wouldn't

be interrupted by Mum constantly going

on. I knew where there was an old sheet,

which Mum and Dad used to cover

furniture if they were doing DIY

in the house. I had a _much_

better use for it, so put it in a

bag, along with the cardboard and paint I'd

found the day before.

At lunchtime, Nish and Tessa agreed

to help me paint the signs. We took the bag

of materials to a corner of the playground

behind the bike sheds, where we wouldn't

Nish on lookout duty

Tessa on spelling

Me, the artist

be disturbed. I spread the sheet and bits of cardboard out on the ground. It took us a while to agree what slogans we wanted, but we decided, and then let our creativity flow . . .

We painted WE NEED NATURE and SAVE THE WILDLIFE on the cardboard, and STOP THE OFFICES! HANDS OFF THE BRAMBLE FIELD! on the big sheet. We stood back to admire our work.

'They look great! Well done, team!' I exclaimed, high-fiving my friends.

'We'd better pack up,' said Tessa. 'Break's

nearly over.'

I picked up the cardboard signs, trying

not to smudge the paint too much. Nish

pulled up the sheet. 'Oops . . . look at this.' The

tarmac under the sheet had a message on it

too. 'TOP OF ICE! AND OF

THE RAM!' Nish read. 'Some of the

paint's come through the sheet, Max.'

'Top of ice and of the ram. It sounds

like something from a poem. Or a riddle,'

I said, thoughtfully.

'It doesn't make sense, Max—like you!'

Nish sniggered.

Come on, you two—get moving! said

Tessa. Painting slogans on the playground

spells big trouble.

TOP OF ICE!

AND OF THE

RAM !

'That really does make sense!' I agreed.

There was a little gap between the bike sheds

and the dinner hall, and we quickly hung

the banners up there to dry, where no one

would notice them. We sneaked off, making

sure no teachers had seen us.

'Remember to wash the paint off

your hands!' I urged my friends.

'We don't want to be caught red-

handed!'

During afternoon lessons I worried that

Trail of evidence

the headteacher would

burst into the room at any

minute and accuse me of

painting graffiti; it would

be just my luck. And just

how exactly would someone

remove paint off tarmac? Would the rain

wash it off? At least only some of the letters

had come through the sheet, so no one would

guess it was to do with the campaign.

I was relieved when the day was over. I
nipped back to the bike shed to bundle the
banners into my bag, and got them home
undetected. I went online, and once I'd found
some biscuits, I was ready to do some
serious research.

Internet cookies

I found loads of interesting stuff about how **important** natural areas are, especially in towns, and how many species were threatened with extinction. I also read about how being in wild places is essential for us, and that made total sense to me. The times when I'd been birdwatching with Dad, or just spent time on the Bramble Field on

RUSTLE

RUSTLE

my own, were some of the times I'd felt the happiest and most relaxed. **Everyone needs nature!**

Online research can take you in all sorts of directions (all of which need biscuits). I learnt that **climate change** is also affecting wildlife all over the world, and I found out that air travel is bad for the climate. **Really bad.** I tried to distract myself by playing Gerbil Hero! 2 on my computer, which worked

for a while, but my mind was working

overtime now.

I went to bed still fretting about flying

and climate change, and I lay awake thinking

about it for ages. I don't remember falling

asleep, but I must have done, because soon

I was dreaming. I was on the flamingo lilo

again, but this time the pool wasn't filled with

lemonade, but with dirty, oily water. A dead

tree-trunk floated into view, with an angry-

looking polar bear clinging to it; the bear

was saying something to me, but I couldn't

understand it. A lobster appeared, and

deflated my lilo by nipping a hole in it with its

pincers. I felt like I was sinking, sinking . . .

I woke up the next

morning feeling really

drained, but sure of one

thing—I really didn't want to

go on holiday if it meant flying. It would have

been good to talk to Mum and Dad about my

worries, but they were trying to give Lily her

breakfast, which as usual seemed to involve

wrestling over bits of soggy bread, and it

wasn't a good time for a chat. In any case, I

needed to get going as I wanted to take my

new banners to the Bramble Field. I wolfed

down a bowl of Corny Snowflakes, grabbed

the bag of banners, and quickly left the

house.

Bag full of banners

Belly full of brekkie

I walked to the Bramble Field, trying to put thoughts about the holiday and **climate change** out of my mind. When you're trying to **save the planet,** it seems there's always something to worry about. The best way I've found to get over my worries is to take action—and right now I needed to

get busy saving the Bramble Field.

    I branched off my usual route to school,

diverting down Meadow Lane. The new fence

dominated one side of the road, standing in

front of the Bramble Field like a hideous spot

on the face of a friend. It needed covering

up! I looked around nervously, but as usual

the road was quiet. I took my banner out of

the bag and tied it to the fence with bits of

string, then did the same with the cardboard

47

placards. **They looked great!** I took

loads of photos on my phone, then continued

on my way, happy with my work.

**295.2mb
of banners**

I found my friends in the playground and showed them my photos of the banners. 'The campaign has been launched!' I announced proudly.

'What happens now?' asked Tessa. 'The office builders won't stop because of a few banners.'

'This is just the start!' I explained. 'I'm working on a plan—there's a lot going on in here,' I said, tapping my head. 'I want to make the school more wildlife-friendly as well. We planted those trees to make a **Forest of Hope** here a while ago, but we need more! Like a pond, or a wildflower area!'

'You'll need to persuade Mr Costive!' said Nish.

'That's the first bit of my plan!' I smiled.

My headteacher is really hard to get hold

of when you need to get him to do something

important, yet he always seems to appear

if you happen to be doing something he

doesn't like. I considered deliberately doing a

cheeky bit of bad behaviour, so he'd

pop up to tell me off, and then I could explain

my ideas, but that was risky. He'd be less likely

to listen to my plans if he was angry with me

(and anyway, I get told off enough as it is).

I spent the rest of lunchbreak looking for

him and was about to give up when I spotted

Mr Costive hurrying across the playground.

I ran over towards him; he saw me coming,

and abruptly turned around, disappearing into

the shed where they keep the bins.

Terrible pong

**Mr Costive's new office?
Maybe I could make him a sign?!**

I got there just as he was closing the door.

'Ah, Max,' he sighed. 'I was just ... er ... making sure the bin lids were on properly. All fine. Goodbye.' He left the bin shed, and started to walk off briskly.

'Hang on, sir!' I said. 'I need to talk to you. I want to rewild Jedley School! I have an idea ...'

'I don't have time for your tomfoolery!' he exclaimed. 'Rewilding? The children here are quite wild enough! Anyway, I'm busy investigating some graffiti that's appeared. Some nonsense about ice and rams. Unacceptable! I don't suppose you know anything about that?' He stared hard at me.

I thought carefully. 'That doesn't make sense, sir,' I said, which wasn't a lie. 'While you're checking the bins, we could do with more space for recycling, by the way.'

(First rule of difficult questions: change the subject. I'd learnt this from watching politicians on TV.)

Never mind that! Mr Costive said, spikily. I'm busy, and you should be in lessons! He strode off.

I trudged back towards the classroom, downhearted. I bumped into my class teacher Ms Perkins in the corridor.

Excuse me, Miss! I need you to talk to Mr Costive. He won't listen to me.

I told her about my ideas to make

the school more wildlife-friendly, and what

I'd learnt about the importance of wild

spaces, and even ended up telling her all

about the threat to the Bramble Field.

There was a lot to tell.

'Whoa, Max!' she said, holding up her hand. Mr Costive's a busy man. I can see you're really into this stuff, but I haven't got time to talk about it now either. I certainly agree that we need to appreciate nature—I'll give it some thought. Now, it's time for lessons!

I sighed, and picked up my workbook.

Why does school always get in the way of the

important stuff?

When lessons finally ended and I got home,

Mum and Dad were in the kitchen with Lily,

making tea. 'Ah, Max! said Mum, with a look

that told me to be on my guard. 'What have

you been doing in the cupboard? There's stuff

all over the floor, and cardboard everywhere.

Were you planning to clear it up?'

To be honest, I hadn't been. 'Sorry . . . I'll tidy it later.'

'Well, make sure you do! Anyway, I got you something.' She rummaged in a bag that was on the table. 'Here! I remembered that you'd grown out of your old swimming trunks, so I got you these!' I held the new trunks at arm's length—they were

HIDEOUS.

Bright pink, with fluorescent orange spiders on them, and 'BEACH BUM!' written across the back. Even Lily was looking at them suspiciously, and she's got terrible taste.

'There's NO WAY I'm ever wearing those, they're horrible!' I exclaimed. 'And why have they got spiders all over them?'

'They're octopuses, not spiders,' replied Mum, huffily. 'I thought they were cheerful. And they were on sale.

HA
HA
HA

You'll need some new trunks for our holiday.'

'Cheerful?' I repeated, shaking my

head. 'Anyway, I wanted to talk to you about

that,' I said, dropping the spider-trunks on the

table. 'I don't think we should take a flight. It's

really bad for the climate!'

Dad looked up. 'Don't

start, Max. We haven't had

a proper holiday for ages,

and one plane trip isn't a big

deal.'

'It all matters!' I exclaimed. 'We said we were going to do what we could to make a difference! Anyway, I've got a better plan. Why don't we have a holiday at home? No need to fly, and much cheaper! I read about it—it's called a staycation. I've got a few ideas...'

'I'm sure you have!' said Dad quickly. 'Let's not hear them now, OK? It's nearly time for tea, anyway.'

'But I'll organize everything—we could

have a great time at home!' I protested. 'I'm really good at making great plans.'

They were both looking at me like I'd suggested eating soap. 'Max, your plans usually lead to trouble, and always cause a mess,' sighed Mum, gesturing at the cupboard.

'Sometimes we need to get away from all that nonsense.'

'Yes, staying at home doesn't sound like much of a holiday to me, Max,' added Dad.

'We can talk more about this later.'

I wasn't getting anywhere, and I was annoyed by what Mum had said. I'd show them, and come up with a plan which would change their minds! I turned to go to my bedroom.

'If you're going upstairs, take your new trunks!' said Mum, but I pretended not to hear.

STOMP
STOMP

I set off for school the next day, meeting

Nish and Tessa as usual. 'Let's make a little

diversion,' I suggested. 'I want to go and

check on the Bramble Field and

see if anything's changed.'

'I don't think we should,

**Time on the wrist?
Old school!
And late FOR school!**

Max,' said Tessa. 'We'll be late unless we get a move on.'

'It'll be fine! It won't take long!' I retorted.

'You always say that before you make us late,' said Nish, looking at his watch and frowning.

'OK—we don't all need to go. I'll have a quick look and catch you up, and report back!'

Nish and Tessa went off towards school,

and I hurried down the side road towards the

site. It wasn't long before I rounded a corner

and saw the harsh gleam of the fence.

But where were my banners? They were

missing—had they been stolen? As I got

closer, I saw them in a pile on the edge of the pavement. Someone had ripped them off the fence and dumped them here.

Who would do that? I picked up my banners, damp from the grass, and wondered what to do next. Should I put them back up?

As I stood there, I saw something moving on the other side of the fence. Then, two men in fluorescent yellow jackets and hard hats came into view. They were carrying clipboards and talking as they moved around the site. I felt a stab of panic. Who were they,

and what was going on?

Then one looked over and saw me. I stood

there, frozen to the spot. He said something

to his mate, and then turned and started

stomping over towards me. I nearly turned

and ran, but I hadn't done anything wrong—

and anyway, if I stayed put I might find out

what they were up to.

Morning! he said, surprisingly cheerfully.

Are those your banners?

I needed to find out what I

could from him without letting

him know too much about my

plans. This required careful

strategy. Fortunately, I had years

of practice at dealing with teachers and parents to draw on . . .

'I saw them on the ground,' I replied (which didn't answer his question, but wasn't even a lie). 'I was just, er . . . wondering what's going on here?'

'It's a development—it'll be an office block,' he said, pointing at the shiny sign. His hard hat was slightly too big, and it wobbled as he spoke, which made it hard to take him seriously. 'Why—what's your interest?'

'Oh, nothing really,' I said as casually as I could. 'When will the building start?'

'A couple of weeks, hopefully,' said the man.

'What!' I exclaimed, not at all casually. That's really soon! Who decided that? What about all the wildlife here?

He sighed. 'It's hardly the Amazon rainforest, is it? Scrappy little sites like this are better used for something that makes

$ $ $

money, if you ask me. Anyway, I don't make

the decisions. I'm only doing my job.'

'But . . .' I started, but he cut me off.

'I should get back to work, and I reckon

you should be in school. Goodbye.'

He smiled politely, but

insincerely, and turned

away. I watched him go,

hard-hat wobbling, and

tension churned in my

belly like a snake.

S-s-s-save the brambles, Max.

And get some s-s-s-salt and
vinegar crisps whilst you're at it.

I walked to school, fuming! A couple of

weeks! Was that all we had to save the

Bramble Field?

I was only just on time, and Ms Perkins

scowled at me when I slipped into the

classroom while she was calling the register.

At the end, she called me over.

Try to get here earlier, Max.
Anyway, no need to look so
worried—I've got something
that will cheer you up. I know you're
keen to make the school more wildlife-
friendly and, as it's such a nice day, I thought
we could have an outdoor learning lesson!
We'll learn about wildlife, and do a practical
activity. Right up your street!

She was right—it did make me feel

better. I was really looking forward to the

outdoor learning session for the rest of the

morning.

After lunchbreak, Ms Perkins led us all

out through the playground and onto the

school field, next to the trees we'd planted

last term. It felt good to be out in the sunny

afternoon. She'd put little mats on the grass

for everyone to sit on, and we

settled down and started

the lesson.

She handed out some info sheets about

the environment, and we all started to read.

It was very interesting, and I was getting into

it . . . until I got distracted by a huge beetle

scampering through the grass next to me. It

was about as big as one of Lily's fingers, with

shiny black wing-cases, like a little jewel.

Wow! I put my hand in the beetle's path,

and it ran onto my palm,

and stopped there,

quivering as if sniffing

out its new surroundings.

I leaned over to nudge Nish. 'Hey, look at this!' I whispered, dropping it onto the mat next to him. I thought he'd be interested, but I wasn't expecting what happened next. He yelped as if he'd been bitten and jumped to his feet, although the beetle hadn't even touched him.

What is that?! he yelled, jigging round like the beetle was in his

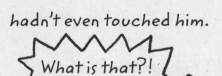

Hi

pants, not on his mat. 'Get rid of it!'

'Nature can be harsh, Nish, remember?'
I grinned.

Of course, everyone was staring at us
now and sniggering.

'What's wrong, Nish?' Ms Perkins called
out.

'He's freaking out, Miss. Something's

bugging him!' I said, and everyone

laughed.

'It's just a beetle—stop being a cry-baby!' shouted Matt

McDonald.

I could tell that Nish

was not amused. I grabbed the

beetle from his mat, holding it carefully

between my hands. 'I'll just

get rid of this, Miss,'

I explained, walking

over to the trees where I could release it.

'Fancy being so scared of a harmless

insect!' I heard someone say.

Snug as a bug . . .

I felt bad for Nish now. I looked

back and could see Nish was

mortified. I thought of a way I could

make things better. I'd always fancied

myself as an actor . . .

I approached the tree, gently

dropping the beetle into the long

grass. Then, I dropped to the ground

Wink, wink

myself with a groan, as if I'd been shot. 'It's not harmless!' I croaked. 'It's a murder-beetle!' I rolled around theatrically, moaning.

'For goodness' sake, Max!' Ms Perkins strode over. 'Stop messing about, and go and sit down!'

'But Miss ... the murder-beetle bit me ...' I whined dramatically.

'I know that you know that I know this is total nonsense, Max,' she said. 'Get up and sit down NOW!'

I picked myself off the ground and sheepishly returned to the class, which was in uproar. It took Ms Perkins a while to restore order and carry on with the lesson.

At the end, she tapped me on the shoulder. 'I'm disappointed in you, Max. I really wanted this outdoor learning session to be a success, because I know how important being in nature is for children. I thought you'd be keener than anyone, and I'm really surprised you were so disruptive.'

'I'm sorry, Miss!' I blurted out. 'I was just trying to take the heat off Nish.'

She sighed. 'I know you mean well, but you really need to think before you act. You'll do much better if you do. OK, I'll see you tomorrow.'

I was bothered by Ms Perkins telling me off,

but I had to put it out of my mind—I had

much more important things to think about.

I discussed it with my friends as we walked

home.

'We need to work out what to do about

the Bramble Field,' I said. 'We've only got a couple of weeks! Learning about wildlife is great, but it's pointless if some whiffhead just builds stupid office blocks on top of all the local wildlife!'

Tessa said, More people need to know about it, Max. Banners aren't enough. It needs to be on the internet as well. And if you could get the newspaper or TV interested . . .

'You're right!' I exclaimed. 'We need to hold an event, and get loads of people there. A protest!'

'I've never been to a protest,' said Nish, dubiously. 'What will we do? How does it work?'

He and Tessa were looking at me expectantly. 'Er . . . well, we make a leaflet, and put it on social media, and tell people to come. And we'll get it on the TV, so the office-building people will see that everyone's against it.'

Tessa looked thoughtful. 'Worth a try,' she said. 'But will it get us into trouble, like when you got everyone to walk out of school last term?'

'That was great, and totally worth it!'
I proclaimed. 'And it was a while ago, and
I haven't been in trouble since, mostly. But
there'll be no trouble if we do it at the
weekend!'

'That's really soon,' said Nish.

'Yes, so we'd better get on with it!' I
scowled. It will have to be Sunday, because
I'm doing family things on Saturday. Let's say
lunchtime. I'll phone the newspaper and get
them to come!'

'Will they take you seriously?' asked

Tessa. 'We're just kids. They might not listen

to us.'

'They should!' I objected. But Tessa did

have a point.

'We need a snappy name for the

campaign,' she suggested. 'To make it sound

more official.'

Now, that was a good idea. We all walked

in silence for a while, thinking. I could almost

hear the cogs turning.

'I've got it!' I cried. 'We will be

POOP – People Opposed
to Office Plans.'

'I'm not sure that sounds official,' said

Nish. 'But it has a ring to it.'

'Yes—people will remember the name.

POOP sticks in the mind!' I said. 'I'll do

a leaflet and we can hand it out at school.

Tessa, I've got a job for you too. You could set

up a page for POOP on Datakrunch and

publicize it there.'

'Sure!' Tessa smiled; she's always on social media. 'We'll make it go viral!'

So, over the next few days POOP burst into action. I made a leaflet advertising the protest on Dad's printer, and Nish helped me hand them out at school. I phoned the newspaper and told them all about it, and they promised to send a reporter.

Tessa posted it all over the internet. We were spreading the word!

It was an especially busy time for me because I had something else to plan as well. The whole holiday business was still preying on my mind—I really didn't want to fly, and it seemed especially wrong to go away when we had so little time to save the Bramble

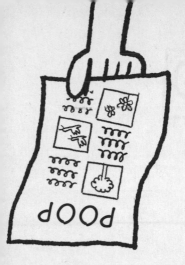

Field. I needed to persuade Mum and Dad to choose a staycation so I could be here to campaign. On Saturday I was planning a test-run. It was going to be quite a weekend!

I was up early on Saturday, because it was
going to be an important day. Dad had
already taken Lily to the park and Mum was
having a lie-in, so I had time to do some
preparation. I didn't know how long I'd have
before they appeared, so I rushed around

getting everything ready. It was hectic,

but I was on a mission, and things were

taking shape.

I'd managed to do most of the things

on my list by the time I heard Mum coming

My to do list:

- ☐ Invent Luxury Cocktail
- ☐ Special Dinner (no lobsters)
- ☐ Tropical Time Zone
- ☐ Palm Trees (too much work?)
- ☐ Organize Cabaret (write song!!)
- ☐ Dress to Impress
- ☐ Wake Mum

downstairs. I greeted her as she entered the kitchen. 'Bonjour! Welcome to Max's hotel, for MAXimum luxury!' I announced. 'Would you care for a cocktail, madam?'

'What on earth are you up to?' demanded Mum, rubbing her eyes. 'And look at the state of the kitchen!'

'I'm doing a little test-run for

Dad's suit jacket and cycling gloves

Mum's holiday hat and shades

the staycation!' I explained. 'Why don't you come and relax with a special drink. On the house, madam! I'll finish tidying up while you drink it.'

'This is ridiculous!' muttered Mum.

'You've got 10 minutes to sort the kitchen out. Meanwhile, I'm going back to bed.' She shuffled slowly upstairs, with a sigh.

Serious Bed head

I started to clean up, but soon heard the

sound of Dad opening the front door. I rushed

to meet him. 'Aloha!' I smiled, beckoning him

in.

He looked at me suspiciously. 'What's

going on?' he asked. 'And why are you

wearing sunglasses and

that ludicrous hat?'

We're in

holiday mode!

I explained. 'Please

put your luggage

down and make yourself comfortable.'

'Your sister is not luggage,' Dad said,

placing Lily in her high-chair.

Mum appeared at the bottom of the

stairs. 'It seems we're trialling a staycation,'

she told Dad, eyebrows

raised.

'Yes!' I exclaimed.

'Here, try a cocktail.'

'What's this?' asked

Dad, sniffing it suspiciously.

'Tropical fruit cocktail!' I announced. 'Try it!'

He gave a cautious sip, and screwed his face up. 'Yuk! What are these weird chunks floating in it? And is that . . . lettuce? And what's the powder in the bottom of the glass?'

'The chunks are tomato—not very tropical, but at least they are fruit. The lettuce is a decorative garnish. It's baking powder at the bottom—I thought it needed more fizz,' I explained.

'Baking powder!'

exclaimed Mum. She poured

her drink down the sink,

shaking her head.

'Don't worry—there's more if

you want some later,' I said, pointing at the

large jug I'd made. Mum stared at the empty

bottle next to the jug.

'Hang on—you used a whole bottle

of Lily's squash to make this muck?' she

exclaimed. 'Honestly, Max!'

'Let's have a nice cup of tea!' said Dad quickly, putting his glass down and switching the kettle on.

'Whatever you like, sir!' I said. 'Perhaps you'd like to relax on the beach, and I'll bring you your tea?'

Dad looked confused—after all, we don't live anywhere near a beach. Well, not usually . . .

I pointed through the window. 'Step this way!' He shrugged at Mum, who was making tea, and followed me into the garden.

'You relax on the beach and sunbathe,' I

said, pointing at where I'd laid a towel over

Lily's sandpit.

I don't think I'll get a suntan he sighed,

glancing at the concrete-grey sky as he

lowered himself down onto the towel.

I headed inside to bring him his tea.

He'd only just sat down when he jumped

up again with a yelp. I turned to see him

throwing the towel over his shoulder and

scrabbling in the sandpit, using

words he'd tell me off

for if I said them.

'Oww!

I sat on this!

A locomotive up

the bum is NOT

relaxing!' he shouted, holding up one of Lily's toy trains.

'Sorry, sir,' I said earnestly. 'Plastic pollution is a problem on beaches everywhere—even in the best resorts.'

'I've had enough of this nonsense!' he yelled. 'I'm going inside, and YOU are going to tidy this up, and then clean the kitchen. OK?'

It didn't sound like I had a choice. I sighed, took off my hat and shades, and set to work.

It took me almost as long to tidy up as it

had done to set up my staycation in the first

place. I was just about finished when Mum

came into the kitchen.

'That's better. Almost back to normal.

Are you ready for some lunch?' she asked.

'Aha! I have that covered, madam!'

I announced, putting my holiday hat and

shades back on again. 'Here's

something I prepared

earlier.' I went over to the

fridge and took out a dish,

placing it in the microwave.

'OK ... **NOT** back to normal,'

muttered Mum, running her hands through

her hair. 'What on earth have you made?'

'It's a tropical vegetable curry,'

I explained. 'It will be ready in five minutes.

Take a seat.'

'I'm not at all sure about this,' Mum

complained, but I persuaded her to get some

plates out and sit down.

The microwave pinged; I served up the

curry, and called Dad for lunch.

'Tropical curry!' I

announced proudly. Dad

surveyed his plate. 'It looks more

like tropical slurry! What's in it?'

Mum prodded at her plate with a fork.

'I'm seeing baked beans, peanuts and raisins,'

she said. 'I don't think they're tropical, Max.'

'OK, I'm going in. Nice knowing you,' said

Dad with a wink, and tried a mouthful.

He chewed slowly, wincing slightly. He swallowed with a grimace, and put down his fork. 'It's gritty, bitter and just weird; and it doesn't taste of curry,' he said, shaking his head. 'Sorry, Max, but I'm not eating this. And surely you didn't put coffee in it?'

'Yes. And cocoa powder. To make it taste exotic,' I explained.

Mum pushed away her plate, untouched.

'I'll make some sandwiches,' she said curtly.

Dad was clearing the plates of curry

away, but suddenly froze. 'That

can't be the time!' he

exclaimed, staring at the clock

on the wall. 'I need to get to the

shops in town before they close today!'

'How did it get so late?' asked Mum.

'Go on, get a move on!'

'I'll take the car,' said Dad. 'Don't you

dare say I should cycle, Max—I'll never get

there in time!' He snatched the car keys and

his phone from the shelf, and headed towards

the door—but then stopped to stare at his

phone.

'Hang on . . . my phone says

it's only half-past one!' he

said, scratching his head.

'Mine too,' said Mum.

'The clock must be

wrong. That's a relief.'

It was time for me to own up. 'Er . . . I

changed the time on the clock,' I confessed.

'I thought that if I changed it to tropical

time, it might feel like we were abroad.'

'For goodness' sake, Max! Well, I might as

well go to the shops now. Bye!'

I ate a sandwich with Mum and helped

clean away the tropical curry. I sensed that

my parents needed a break from my holiday

experiment, so decided to retreat to my room

before Dad got back. I checked Datakrunch,

and was excited to see that lots of people

had shared POOP's posts, and were

saying they were coming to the protest

tomorrow. That really cheered me up.

It's easy to spend ages on social media

without noticing. Time passed, and I realized

I needed to complete my staycation test-run

before it got too late. I put on my holiday

hat and shades, and then made the supreme

sacrifice: I put on the hideous

spider-trunks to complete

the outfit. If that didn't get them in the

holiday spirit, nothing would! I found Lily's

little toy guitar, and headed downstairs.

Mum and Dad were in the kitchen.

Mum sighed when she saw

me. 'Here we go again ...'

she muttered, but then

brightened when she

noticed the spider-

trunks. 'Oh! I'm glad you

like your new trunks!'

I ignored Mum's comment and clapped my hands for attention. 'At Max's hotel, we provide holiday entertainment for all our honoured guests! Please be seated, and enjoy the show!'

I cleared my throat, strummed the guitar, and started to sing:

'It's staycation time

We're feeling fine

We don't need to fly away.

Lobsters freak me out

I have no doubt

At home it's best to stay.

I love the trees,

and the birds and bees

Let's have a natural holiday.

I'm feeling glad

With Mum and Dad,

And Lily, by the way.'

I bowed, which made my hat fall off, but I didn't mind. I looked up, and instead of the tired and exasperated looks my parents had been giving me all day long, they were both grinning.

'Bravo!' said Dad, clapping and laughing. 'Did you write that yourself? Silly question. It's great!'

'Yes!' Mum laughed. 'You've got a great voice! Maybe a little work needed on the guitar playing, though . . .'

'OK, show us how it's done!' I grinned,

passing her the guitar.

That was the start of a really fun evening.

Mum had a go at playing tunes

on the tiny guitar, and Dad

got a spoon and a fork

and drummed on the

biscuit tin. I sang,

while Lily did a funny

little jig to the music.

It was like a family band! It was the best

evening we'd had together for a long time,

and it almost did feel like we'd had a little

holiday at home.

THE TWYFORDS!

I Woke up really early on Sunday, excited

because it was the day of the

POOP protest! After breakfast,

Nish and Tessa came round and

we gathered up the banners and

placards we'd made. I had told Mum and Dad

we were off to hang out in the Bramble Field

but I didn't tell the whole story. I couldn't

risk them saying no—the future of the

Bramble Field was too important!

Soon, we set off to the protest.

POOP had hit the streets!

We arrived at the site

and I was disappointed

to see that no one else

was there. 'Where is

everyone?' I complained.

'Chill out, Max!' said Tessa. 'It's only just 1 o'clock now. You're just not used to being on time for anything!'

Maybe she had a point. We tied our banners to the fence and stood by the side of the road with our placards. It wasn't too long before some others arrived—Ryan and Ali from my class, plus Ryan's big sister. Then Rashid and Lianne showed up, and Charlie with his parents, and Chloe, and Mo, and even grumpy Danny Belter. Suddenly, more and more people were arriving, mostly from my school, but some I didn't know. It wasn't just kids—quite a few adults were there, including Ms Perkins, who looked different out of school— less teacherish, and more like a <u>normal</u> <u>person</u>.

'Look! The newspaper's here!' said Nish, pointing at a man holding a huge camera, and a woman with a notepad.

With normal person trainers

'This is great!' I beamed at Nish and

Tessa. 'There's loads of people!'

'What happens now?' asked Nish.

I had to admit that was a good question.

I hadn't really thought of that ...

'We need a speech,'

Big camera means big close-up!

suggested Tessa. 'There

are always speeches

at protests.'

I nodded, and

realized my friends

were looking at me expectantly.

'You should say something. You've done speeches before!' said Tessa.

'But . . . I haven't prepared anything. What do I say?' I stammered.

'Whatever comes into your head, as usual!' grinned Nish. 'Go on, Max. You can do it.'

I could see people getting restless, and I was worried they'd leave if nothing happened soon. I took a deep breath, stood on a tree stump, and started to speak.

Excuse me, everyone! I'm going to do

a little speech!

People gathered round,

and the photographer

trained his lens on me.

I tried to forget my

nerves.

'Thank you all

for coming! I'm Max,

from POOP.

We're against the office building, because
this is the Bramble Field, and it's really
important for wildlife. Species everywhere
are becoming extinct because of humans,
and I want it to stop!'

There was a little cheer. This was going
OK! I continued.

Mo

Chloe

Ali

Ryan

Ryan's big sister ♡

Charlie and
his parents

Danny Belter

Rashid

Lianne

Not sure who this is?!

'The field might not look

much to you, but I love it here—

there's birds, and trees and wildflowers,

and amazing big spotty newts in

the ponds that look like baby

dinosaurs! It's special, and we must

save it. The world needs more trees

and newts, not offices full of

desks and people in suits!'

'Trees and newts, not desks and suits!'

shouted Nish, and everyone cheered.

Some of the kids in my class started chanting, and 'Trees and newts, not desks and suits!' echoed across the field. Everyone was laughing and clapping, and the photographer was snapping away. I jumped down from the tree stump.

TREES AND NEWTS, NOT DESKS AND SUITS!

Ms Perkins walked over. 'I enjoyed your speech, Max. I can see this really matters to you—well done! I'm off now. See you in the morning.'

I looked around. Other people were leaving too, and the kids from my class came over to say goodbye. Things were quietening down.

'What happens now?' asked Nish.

Before I could answer, the newspaper reporter came over. Is the protest over? she asked.

I surveyed the scene. Apart from my friends, the only people left were Mo and Ryan milling about at the side of the road, and Danny, who stood staring through the fence at the Bramble Field.

'Er . . . No!' I said. 'POOP do not give up that easily.'

'What will happen next?' enquired the reporter. Why did everyone keep asking me that?

I decided it was up to me to make

something happen. I saw Danny Belter's bike

leaning against the fence, with his bike-lock

hanging on the handlebars. I noticed he'd left

the key in it . . .

I suddenly knew what to do. I grabbed

the lock, and threaded its chain around my

waist and the mesh of the

fence. I snapped the lock

shut, fastening myself to

the fence. It was time

to make a stand!

(Or sit!) ———>

I heard Nish and Tessa gasp, and the

photographer's camera clicking as fast as a

machine gun.

'Oi!' said Danny, rushing over. 'You've

got my lock!'

'Sorry, Danny,' I said. 'You'll get it back.

It's for a good cause!'

 He stared at me for ages with a face like

thunder. 'Just don't lose the key, OK?' He

turned and stomped off, wheeling his bike

grumpily up the road.

136

'This will make a great image!'

proclaimed the reporter. She asked me

my name, what school I went to, and a

few other questions, and then she and the

photographer went back to their car and

sped off. I noticed that Ryan had gone too.

It was just me and my friends now.

Suddenly, it felt really quiet. 'So what happens now?' asked Nish.

'Stop asking that! We wait', I replied. 'I've locked myself to this fence to save the Bramble Field and I'm staying here until it's saved!'

'That could be a while, Max,' said Tessa.

'Everyone else has gone home now. Shouldn't

we call it a day? It's gone really well! We can

always come back.'

I frowned and shook my head.

I'm stopping here. It's the principle

of the thing!

Tessa and Nish both

nodded, but I could tell they

weren't convinced. None of us said

anything for a while.

Tessa broke the silence. 'I'm very sorry, Max, but I'm going to have to go. It's nearly teatime, and I didn't have a proper lunch and I'm really hungry. Are you sure you're staying?'

I nodded. It was the principle of the thing!

'OK . . . well, sorry I can't stay any longer. Good luck! I'll come and see how you're doing soon.' With that, she was off.

'Just you and me, then, eh?' I said to

Nish, cheerfully. He nodded, leaning on the

fence with his hands in his pockets.

Maybe we should have brought something

to do, you know. Like a game or something.

To pass the time he said.

'I didn't think of that', I conceded.

Nish really likes football, but

I couldn't play that right

now. He started pacing

slowly up and down the

fence to one side of me,

scuffing his feet on the ground.

'We could play I Spy?' I suggested,

brightly. 'I'll start. I spy . . . something

beginning with F.'

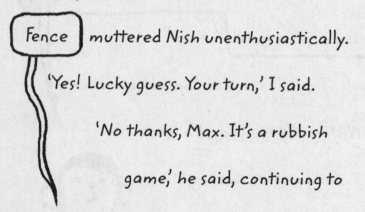

Fence muttered Nish unenthusiastically.

'Yes! Lucky guess. Your turn,' I said.

'No thanks, Max. It's a rubbish

game,' he said, continuing to

pace.

For a while the only

noise was the scuffing

of Nish's shoes on the tarmac. I could tell he was bored, and he wasn't in the mood to keep me entertained, either.

'You know what—I'll be fine here if you want to go,' I said.

'Really?' said Nish, quickly. 'Will you be alright on your own?'

'Of course!' I smiled. 'Go on, go! I'll see you later.'

'If you're sure . . .' said Nish, who was trying not to look relieved, and almost succeeding.

Soon after Nish left, and I was alone. It felt really quiet now. I started wondering what Tessa was having for tea and realized I was starting to feel hungry too. I wished I'd remembered to bring some food. I thought of calling Mum and Dad to ask them to bring me something, but my phone was out of battery. It seemed I really was on my own.

I was getting bored myself now, though I hated to admit it. (Fortunately, there wasn't anyone to admit it to anyway.) Not much happens when you're chained to a fence, it seems.

I could see someone walking towards me

from the end of the road.

Hopefully another

photographer?

I couldn't help

wondering if they'd

Ice-cream microphone!

have any food. I decided that I was going to

demand something to eat if they wanted an

interview, which seemed only fair.

I craned my head for a better view, and

realized it was Tessa. Brilliant! Even better,

when she arrived, she had some sandwiches

she'd made for me, and crisps. I tucked

in greedily.

'Thanks, Tessa—you're a

lifesaver! I'm starving,' I said

between mouthfuls.

'No probs!' she replied.

'I felt bad for you while I was

having my dinner, so thought I'd bring you

something. Oh look—isn't that Nish?'

We peered down the road. There was a

figure a long way away, and it had to be our

friend, with his funny bouncy walk.

When he got to us, I was delighted to see

he'd brought a big bottle of water. I drank it

all in one go—I hadn't realized how thirsty I'd

been.

'It looks like you needed

that!' said Nish. 'Are you ready

to leave, Max? It's getting

dark.'

'It is,' I agreed, 'but I'm staying.

It's the principle of the thing.'

My friends looked uncertain, and I could

see they weren't sure it was a good idea to

stay. Still, they didn't leave this time.

I started to feel an unmistakeable toilet

urge. That water must have gone right

through me. I considered asking

Nish if I could wee in

his empty bottle,

but he'd made sure

to bring a nice

reusable one—and

if I used it as a temporary toilet, no one

would want to reuse it. I tried hard not to

think about it.

My non-wee thoughts were interrupted

by a mournful cry cutting through the fading

light.

It made Nish jump. 'What

was that?'

'Probably an owl,' I guessed. 'It

wouldn't surprise me if there are owls on the

Bramble Field. Maybe bats too. Pretty cool, eh?'

'Bats?' said Tessa sharply. 'It's getting really dark now, and it's spooky here. I think we should go.'

Wait—what's that? asked Nish, pointing up the road. We all saw a weird light bobbing in and out of view. We stood transfixed as the light disappeared and reappeared.

'It's getting closer!' said Tessa. 'Can you hear it?'

I nodded and tried to turn around to get

a better look, making the bike chain rattle.

'Shhh!' she hissed, and we listened

to the eerie wheezing and grinding which

accompanied the strange light.

'It's a ghost!'

whispered Nish. 'Or a maniac with an axe!'

'I don't believe in ghosts,' said Tessa

firmly. I wasn't sure I did either, but noticed I

was gripping the mesh of the fence so tightly

that my sweaty palms hurt.

'We should run!' I shouted. 'Quick, give

me the key!'

All at once the light filled my head,

blindingly bright. I scrunched my eyes shut.

'Too late!' cried Tessa. 'It's here!'

I didn't dare open my eyes. My heart was racing, and even though it was still chilly, I was sweating. I wished I wasn't locked to a fence, so we could all run away. All I could hear was the ghostly wheezing sound, and I was painfully aware of the dazzling light,

even with my eyes closed. I actually thought I
was going to wee myself. Facing a ghost is bad
enough, but facing a ghost with wee in your
pants has got to be worse.

'Er . . . hi, Mr Twyford!' I heard Tessa say.
What?! I opened my eyes. Yes, Dad was there,
sitting on his tandem bike, breathing heavily.

'At last!' he said, switching off his bike light.

'Are you all OK?'

'Yes . . . fine!' I said, more cheerfully than I felt. 'The noise of your bike just freaked us out a bit in the dark, that's all.'

Dad was staring at the chain around my waist. 'Hmmm . . . yes, the mind can play tricks. Right now, for example, it looks as if you've locked yourself to that fence. It must be an illusion, because I know you wouldn't be stupid enough to do that.'

It's a bad sign when Dad decides to be all sarcastic like that—it means he's moving through 'annoyed' and approaching 'really quite angry'.

'Why didn't you tell us what you were up to, Max?' he demanded. 'We were worried about you, and you weren't answering your phone. We were expecting you back ages ago. I don't know what you've been up to out here, but I want you to unlock that chain and come home.'

'Sorry . . .' I muttered. 'Let's

have the key, Nish.'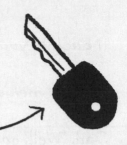

'Er . . . I haven't got it,' he replied.

'I gave it to you!' I exclaimed.

'I didn't want to have it in case I lost

it, remember?'

'Yes . . . but then I gave it to Tessa, in case

I lost it,' explained Nish.

I held out my hand for the

key, but Tessa shrugged. 'I gave

it back to you, Max. Definitely.'

'Let me guess! In case you lost it?' said

Dad. 'Well, now you've ALL lost it! This is

ridiculous!'

'Someone must've dropped it', I said.

'Look on the ground. And hurry up—I need

the toilet!'

The three of them trailed up and down

the fence, using Dad's flickering bike light to

search the ground. I couldn't join

in, being locked to the fence.

All I could think about was

needing a wee. They'd better find

that key soon ...

It was no good—I was desperate. I

started to rotate myself so I was facing the

fence, which was a bit like having a blunt

cheese-grater slowly rolled over my shoulder.

Ow!

'What are you doing, Max?' asked Dad,

looking up from his examination of the grass

verge.

'Toilet manoeuvres!' I explained. 'Don't

look!'

With my back turned to

them, I could wee at last.

I don't mind saying

that I've done a lot of

wees in my life, and

AAAHHHHH

this was definitely the most awkward.

The sense of relief was intense, and I was feeling very pleased with myself—until I felt a dampness on my jeans. I tried to look down, but my nose kept catching in the mesh of the fence. Even in the dark I knew that I'd managed to wee all over my jeans. I groaned, hoping no one would notice.

'Are you OK?' asked Dad, pointing his bike light at me. 'Hey! What's that?' He strode forward, and snatched something out of the back pocket of my jeans. 'The key!'

he said triumphantly, waving it

above his head. 'Honestly,

Max!'

'I told you I gave it to

you!' said Tessa, while Dad

unlocked the chain. I felt like a fool—a fool

with wee on his jeans. I stepped stiffly away

from the fence into the shadows, hoping no

one would notice the wet patches.

Unfortunately, Dad noticed. 'Oh dear,

Max. I think you missed,' he said.

Well, your protest certainly made a splash! Nish tittered.

'I couldn't help it, whiffhead!' I blurted out indignantly. I was blushing so hard I was sure my face must be glowing in the dark.

Nish's merriment stopped when he saw I was upset. 'Sorry, Max. I bet it's not easy to go when you're locked to a fence.'

165

'Yes, don't worry, Max,' added Dad quickly. 'These things happen. Now, let's get you all home.'

We collected up our banners and trooped off with Dad as he pushed his tandem. After dropping off Nish and Tessa, Dad and I finally made it home. After a shower and some toast I just wanted to go to bed. Mum and Dad had a LONG chat with me about being responsible and always telling them what I'm doing and the importance of not chaining myself to fences. I was so tired I just

nodded along. Eventually Mum steered me up

to bed. She asked me if I thought the protest

was worth it. Had it gone well? Right then I

was so exhausted I just didn't know.

I woke up the next day much too early, and

still feeling tired. I knew I wouldn't get back

to sleep, so I dragged myself out of bed and

went downstairs.

Dad was in the kitchen. 'Ah, Max! Good

morning. Up early to avoid the autograph-hunters?' he grinned.

This made no more sense than most of his 'jokes'. 'What are you on about?' I frowned.

'It seems you're famous—for fifteen minutes, at least.' He pushed a copy of the local paper across the table. The headline was

BRAVE BOY BIDS TO BLOCK BUILDING ON BRAMBLE FIELD

Underneath was a big picture of ME

chained to the fence. The article went on

to report what I'd said about the wildlife on

the site.

'Well done, Max,' said Dad. 'I'm not

generally a big fan of you locking yourself

to things, but it looks like it worked this

time. You've really got your

campaign in the news.'

He was right. I hadn't been sure what to expect this morning, but this was really positive. Yesterday had been a success, and I felt a warm glow—POOP was really getting somewhere!

I poured myself a bowl of Corny Snowflakes, and Dad gave me his phone so I could read the online version of the newspaper article, and then post it on Datakrunch. Everyone was going to hear about it now!

Soon, loads of people were sharing the article!

When I arrived at school, someone shouted, 'Who's a brave boy then?' and everyone laughed. A crowd gathered round me, firing off questions about the protest,

and asking what it felt like being locked to

a fence. I told them all about it (missing out

the bit where I weed on my jeans).

I noticed Danny Belter

staring at me <u>intense</u>ly, like

a stroppy owl up past its

bedtime. I broke away

from the group, and walked

hesitantly over to him.

'Hi, Danny . . . here's your bike-lock,' I

said, fishing it out of my bag. 'I'm sorry I took

Nice and clean

it without asking, but . . . I

needed it.'

I braced myself for a serious outpouring

of grump, but to my surprise, none came.

'It's OK,' he said. 'I love that place, you

know. I hang out there sometimes, and it

makes me feel . . . happy. I hope you save it.'

He nodded solemnly, and walked off.

I was gobsmacked. I'd never have guessed

that Danny liked to go there too. If the

Bramble Field could make him happy, there

really must be something special about the place!

The day went well, with kids congratulating me, and talking about the newspaper story. I felt proud that everyone was inspired by the campaign. Well, nearly everyone . . . as I was leaving at the end of the day, I heard an all-too-familiar voice cut across the playground. 'Max Twyford! A word, please!' I sighed, and turned to see the headteacher looming into view.

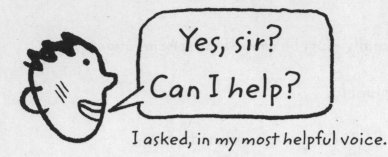

Yes, sir? Can I help?

I asked, in my most helpful voice.

'You can help by not bolting yourself to

street fittings! You're all over the newspapers.

Unacceptable!'

'But it was the

weekend, not school

time!' I objected.

'I strongly disapprove

of meddling with fencing

at any time, Max. It reflects badly on Jedley School. Do I make myself clear?'

'Yes, sir,' I muttered, watching as he strode off.

I set off for home with my friends, and soon forgot about Mr Costive.

'So, how does it feel to be an eco-hero?' grinned Nish. 'Your picture will be up with all those others you showed us!'

'I'm not sure about that,' I laughed. 'Anyway, being some kind of hero isn't important—saving the Bramble Field is what

matters. See you tomorrow!'

As soon as I got home, I checked

Datakrunch, and it was crazy. My post

had been shared all over the place, and it

had  448 likes! There were loads

of comments too—some really positive, but

some less so, and a few just nasty. It made my

head spin to try and read them all, so I gave

up, and just looked at the likes. A couple of

hours later, I had 602. By the time

I went to bed, it was up to nearly

800!

It was hard to get to sleep after spending

the evening on Datakrunch. I lay awake,

thoughts wriggling around my head

like a handful of worms in an old sock.

I tried to forget the hostile comments I'd read, but that was easier said than done. I thought of my hundreds of likes, but that started to feel hollow too. Did they actually mean anything? Even if I got a billion likes on social media, if they built those offices in the real world, I'd have failed.

I went down to breakfast the next day feeling

tired and flat. Dad came into the kitchen.

'Good morning, Mr Celebrity!' he smiled.

'How are we doing today?'

'OK,' I shrugged, with a mouth full

of cereal. I didn't feel like a

celebrity, and I didn't want to be one. Dad

obviously guessed that I wasn't in the mood

for talking, and so he let me be. I polished off

my breakfast and left for school.

It was great that everyone was talking

about the Bramble Field now, but I knew that

it wasn't enough. It felt like the campaign

was only just beginning, and I needed to come

up with a plan for the next stage. I spent the

morning's lessons turning over ideas in my

mind, but wasn't getting anywhere.

After lunch I ran out into the playground

with all the others, but it wasn't long before

Ms Perkins came out and found me. 'A quick

word, please, Max.' I exchanged glances with

Nish and Tessa. What was this about?

Don't worry, you're not in

trouble. There's someone here

who wants to meet you.

'Is it someone from the newspaper

again?' I asked, doubtfully.

'No, more interesting than that!

Come with me.'

I followed her back to her classroom. A woman was waiting there, wearing a wide-brimmed hat perched on top of her curly hair. She had a little flower in the lapel of her jacket, and smiley eyes.

'Ah! You must be Max. I'm Holly Pooter. I study pond life, so was especially keen to meet you. I read all about the protest

against the new office block, you see, and I

was interested in what you said about newts.

They are my speciality.'

'So, you're like a newt-ologist?' I asked

her.

'You could say that,' she grinned. 'I'm

the chief scientist at Pals of Ponds—we

campaign to protect water-life. So, tell me

about your protest.'

Holly asked me lots of questions about

the Bramble Field, and I told her all about

the wildlife, and especially the newts. I

described them as well as I could—the ridge

along their back and tail,

their warty skin, and the

leopard-spots on their

bellies. Holly listened really

carefully and wrote down

**Holly's big book
of little newts**

what I said. She also got me to draw a map of

the Bramble Field in her notebook, so I could

mark the ponds where I'd seen the newts with

a big cross.

'Perfect! Like a treasure map!' she

beamed. 'Thank you, Max. I'll go and have a

look for myself and see if I can find anything

interesting.'

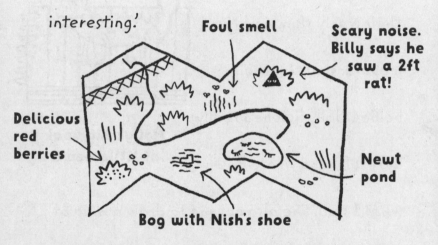

Foul smell

Scary noise. Billy says he saw a 2ft rat!

Delicious red berries

Newt pond

Bog with Nish's shoe

'How will you do that? It's all fenced off

now,' I reminded her.

'Not a problem. Fences do not deter a

qualified newt-ologist!' she replied, with a wink. 'Thanks for your time, Max. You've been really helpful, and I can tell that you've got a really good eye for wildlife. Keep at it!'

With that, she tipped her hat to me and Ms Perkins, and left the classroom.

Talking to her had taken up most of break-time, and it was almost time for lessons again; but I didn't mind, because talking to Holly had been great. We had an actual chief scientist on our side now!

During lessons that afternoon my strong

imagination was working overtime with new

campaign ideas. Thoughts buzzed in my head

like flies bouncing against a window-pane,

 while I pretended to listen

to Ms Perkins.

I couldn't wait till the end of the day

so I could consult my friends. As we walked

home, I told them all about meeting the

newt-ologist.

'So, we're joining forces with Pals of

Ponds!' I announced. 'It's an anti-office

alliance!'

'POOP and POP!' laughed Nish.

'What happens next, then?'

'I'm glad you asked me that . . .' I told

them all about my latest plan, which—even if

I do say so myself—was excellent.

'We'll do a sit-in! We can get Lily's

paddling pool, and put it in the middle of

town. Then, we'll sit in it dressed like newts,

with a banner saying <u>SAVE</u> <u>OUR</u> <u>PONDS</u>!

And we can get Holly there to tell everyone

about pond life, and give out leaflets,' I

explained. 'What do you think?'

'At least no one will notice you have a wee if you're in a paddling pool!' sniggered Nish. I gave him a death-stare, which shut him up.

'Never mind that,' said Tessa quickly. 'How do you dress like a newt?'

'No problem!' I smiled. 'Danny Belter has a dinosaur onesie. We'll borrow that! It's fairly newt-like.'

'He has a dinosaur onesie?' spluttered

Nish. 'How do you know that?'

'His sister posted a pic on Datakrunch. He made her take it down again, but I saw it first.'

'Hmmm . . . Asking the grumpiest person we know to lend us something he'd rather no one knew about? Not going to happen, Max,' said Tessa. 'Especially after you nicked his bike-lock.'

'_Borrowed!_' I protested. 'And he didn't mind.'

We stopped at the corner where our

routes home separated. 'Anyway, I'll think of

something,' I said. 'See you tomorrow.'

That evening, I spent some time trying to

design a newt costume, but didn't get very

far. I wasn't sure I really wanted to dress as a

newt and sit in a paddling pool in town . . . but

I couldn't back down now. It troubled me as I

tried to sleep that night, but the next day was

the end of term and I was soon distracted.

The last day of term is always a good day—

everyone's in a good mood, and the teachers

are relaxed and do fun things in lessons. Even

Mr Costive looked like he might be in danger

of actually smiling.

The last lesson was over, and everyone

spilled out into the sunny playground, ready

for the holidays. I strolled towards the school

gates with my friends, as noisy crowds of

excited kids swarmed about.

Some parents were waiting at the gates,

and I stopped in my tracks when

I saw Holly Pooter amongst

them. What could this mean? She tipped her hat to us, and I introduced her to Nish and Tessa.

'I've got something important to tell you,' she said. 'I did a scientific survey of the ponds you told me about, and I saw your newts. Handsome devils, aren't they? They're great crested newts—the only ones I know of round here, and a protected species!'

'Protected?' repeated Tessa. 'So no one can ever build offices on them?'

'It's a bit more complicated than that,' warned Holly. 'Nothing's safe for ever—we environmentalists always have to be on our guard. But now I've got the site registered as important newt habitat. That means no building can be done while the newts are there, by law. The land is certainly safe for now!'

'So we won't be dressing up like muppets and sitting in a paddling pool after all. Brilliant!' added Nish.

'PHEW!' I cried. My head was spinning—

this was amazing news. The campaign had

succeeded, and POOP had won! I

needed to let everyone know.

Holding my hands high,

I shouted for quiet. Listen,

everyone! I've got some

important news! It took me

a while to get everyone to listen,

but eventually I announced that the

Bramble Field was safe.

'Three cheers for Max!' shouted

Holly suddenly, and HOORAY!
HOORAY! HOORAY!

rang out from the gathered crowd of kids.

Holly Pooter, my
NEWT best friend

**My face
glowing
orange
like my
T-shirt**

It's not just me,' I told her, blushing. 'Loads of people helped—Nish and Tessa, and you, and most of all the newts.'

'Maybe, but it was you that first noticed the site was special,' she said. 'If you hadn't done that, and you hadn't taken a stand at the fence, those newts would be extinct in this area!'

The crowd around the school gates was drifting apart; time to go home. I suggested visiting the Bramble Field on the way. Holly was keen, and she walked with me and my friends, chatting in the sunshine.

Soon we were standing on Meadow Lane,

looking at the site. 'Will they take this down now?' I asked, pinging the mesh of the fence with my finger.

'I hope so,' said the newt-ologist. 'After all, it's not a building site anymore. It ought to be a nature reserve.' We all nodded in agreement.

She looked at her watch. 'I'd better go — someone's found an unusual toad in a hairdresser's drainpipe, and I need to

I was only popping
in for a trim!

check it out. Well, I hope I meet you all again. Keep your eyes open for nature—it's amazing what you'll see that most people miss. Enjoy the holidays!'

Our new friend bustled off down the road. I said goodbye to Nish and Tessa, and set off for home. I felt like I was walking on air all the way. If this was what saving wild places felt like, I wanted more of it!

I couldn't wait to tell Mum and Dad the news. I told them everything when I got in—about the great crested newts, and how rare they were, and the newt-ologist, and how nice she was, and how she'd said I had a fine eye for wildlife. (I was especially pleased about that.) The best thing of all, though, was that the Bramble Field was safe now.

There was a lot to tell, and it took a while.

'Well, that's great news, Max!' said Dad.

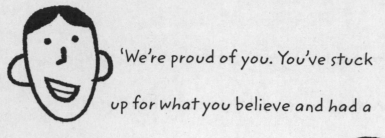 'We're proud of you. You've stuck up for what you believe and had a real success.'

'And you somehow did it all without getting a single detention,' added Mum, with a wink.

'Well done, love! Anyway, school's over now, and it's time to think about our holiday.'

'Yes, we've finally booked our break,' added Dad, reaching over to the pile of brochures.

I felt myself tense up. Everything was great, and I didn't want to spoil it with an argument about holidays and flying again.

'This is where we're going,' said Dad, pushing an open brochure in front of me. There were no pictures of sunny beaches, palm trees, or anything like that; instead there were forests, and mountains, and people in hats and coats around a campfire. 'A camping holiday. We're not going abroad. No flying, Max!'

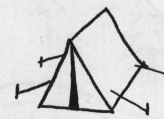

'And definitely no lobsters!' Mum smiled.

'Really?' I asked, tentatively. 'I thought

you really wanted sun?'

'It might be sunny when we go camping,'

suggested Dad hopefully.

'It will probably rain,' said Mum. 'But

that's OK. The campsite looks very nice,

actually, and it's surrounded by miles of

beautiful countryside.

Your dad can take
you birdwatching and
exploring, and there's an

excellent café in the village. That's where I'll
be if it rains.'

I didn't know what to say. I knew how
much they had been looking forward to a
beach holiday.

'Aren't you pleased, Max?' enquired Dad,
noting my silence. 'Don't you think you'll like it?'

'Oh yes, I'll love it,' I replied. 'I just feel a

bit bad you won't get the holiday abroad you wanted.'

'We're happy,' said Mum. 'When you organised that staycation weekend, we were both surprised how much we enjoyed it—in the end! We know you're trying to do the right thing, so we're going to do our bit, too. Besides, with the money we're saving on the flights, we're going to buy a big hammock for the back garden!'

I grinned. 'That's great!' I said. 'I'll tell

you what—I'll even wear my holiday hat and

those spider-trunks you bought me, so we're

all in the mood!'

'You're not doing any cooking, though,'

added Dad, and we all laughed.

Things felt really good. After all, my

friends and I had saved the Bramble Field,

and shown that we could make a real

difference. I reckoned I deserved a holiday!

Have you read . . .

Hi, I'm Max and I'm on a mission to save the planet. I reckon **BIG CHANGE** has to start somewhere so I'm putting my plans into action RIGHT AWAY by:

⌂ Hiding my parents' car keys
(I didn't mean for them to end up in the loo...)

⌂ Inventing my signature vegetarian dish - lettuce pie

⌂ Going to school in my sleeping bag to save on heating

Also packed with <u>REAL</u> tips on saving OUR PLANET.

WALK
& CYCLE MORE

Here are s

And if you need to go far, share your journey.

Cars produce a lot of carbon dioxide. We get happier and healthier when we walk and cycle too. If we share the car or use buses and trains, we pollute the world less.

BUY LESS
& LOOK AFTER WHAT YOU'VE GOT

A lot of modern things are made of oil. For example, all plastic and many of the clothes you wear come from oil products. But one day, the oil will run out.

Think before you buy. Do you really need that new thing? It is better to mend things and swap or share with your friends than to throw them away and buy new

TURN DOWN THE HEAT
& PUT ON A JUMPER

Heating houses produces a lot of carbon dioxide. If we feel cold, we can put on an extra jumper. We can also turn off the radiator and lights when we are not using a room, and turn the TV to standby when we are not watching it.

These pages were written by Mim Saxl, Low Carbon West Oxford & Eleanor Watts, Rose Hill & Iffley Low Carbon

...ings we can all do!

PROTECT NATURE
& PLANT MORE TREES

We need trees because they suck in carbon dioxide and give out oxygen, which we need to breathe! Planting trees and looking after the animals around us is a good thing—and can be a lot of fun!

TALK ABOUT YOUR FEELINGS
& TAKE ACTION

A lot of us feel scared or worried about climate change. It helps to talk about how you feel with family and friends. Maybe they'll want to make some changes too! You could make notices for the playground, ask your parents to walk you to school or write to your MP.

EAT LESS MEAT & DAIRY
& BUY LOCAL FOOD

In many parts of the world, people are cutting down or burning trees so that they can raise animals for meat. Also, cows, sheep, and pigs burp and fart a lot. This produces methane, which is a powerful greenhouse gas!

Some of the story ideas were inspired by the work Kids Climate Action Network are doing.

You can visit the website here: kidsclimateaction.org

Tim Allman grew up in Worcestershire, where he was lucky to live near to a large urban nature reserve, which he spent a lot of his childhood exploring (although he never found any newts.) After studying Botany and Nature Conservation at University, he ran away from his first proper job to join the anti-roadbuilding protests. This led to a decade spent as a full-time environmental activist, and an ongoing commitment to social and environmental change.

Nick Shepherd comes from a small industrial village in Yorkshire, and with the rolling green countryside only a short bike ride away, he would enjoy nothing more than staying indoors, playing video games, and drawing silly characters. Years of study and work later, and not much has changed. Nick is an animal lover; he once rescued two baby squirrels and nursed them back to full health. Now he shares his home and art studio with his cat, who will happily spend the whole day sat on his keyboardddddddddd.